Sam Usher

SNOW

templar publishing

When I woke up
this morning, it
was snowing!

I couldn't wait to
go to the park.

All I needed to do
was dress,

wash, put my
shoes on,

and get Grandad.

We had to get outside
in the snow…

… before anyone else.

I was ready to go,
but Grandad wasn't.

I said, "Don't forget
the snow!"

And he said,
"Don't forget your scarf."

So we weren't quick enough to be first.

Grandad was taking ages.
So I shouted,

"**All** the others will
get there first, Grandad –
DON'T FORGET
THE SNOW!"

And Grandad said,
"Don't forget
your hat!"

So we weren't quick enough
to go with my friends.

Grandad was taking
absolutely **ages**.
So I shouted,

"HURRY UP,
GRANDAD!"

And he said,
"It's okay, we're not
going to miss
the fun."

But we were! I told him **all** the cats and dogs were out there.

Grandad laughed and said the whole zoo
was probably out there.

And then I saw something…

I did!

Finally, Grandad was ready.

We were off to the park.

Where I could have fun with everyone at last.

We played all the games you
can play in the snow.

Grandad won the snowball fight
by six slushings to four.

So I think he had fun too.

Back at home, Grandad and I agreed some things are definitely worth waiting for.

I hope it snows again tomorrow.